This

PLAYDATE KIDS

Book

belongs to:

_____

Chloe   Cosmos   Danny   Dakota

For my grandchildren Brian, Mary, Matthew, Seth, Owen and Clara
and to all the children I've helped for the past 34 years in Malibu, my hometown - A.T.

For Julian - W.M.E.

Copyright ©2006 Playdate Kids Publishing

PO Box 2785
Malibu, CA 90265-9998

ISBN 1-933721-04-9

Library of Congress Control Number 2006901351

Printed in China

Cosmos' Mom and Dad Are Moving Apart

by
Annie Thiel, Ph.D.

illustrated by
William M. Edwards
and
Karen Marjoribanks

PLAYDATE KIDS PUBLISHING
LOS ANGELES

A TENA FANNING
PUBLICATION

Cosmos' mom and dad used to fight all the time.

His parents decided that they would be happier
if they were not married anymore.

"No sweetheart, the divorce doesn't have anything
to do with YOUR behavior," Mom said.
"The divorce is between your father and me."
"That's right," Dad added.
"We're divorcing each other, we're not divorcing you.
We LOVE you!"

"You might feel many things during the divorce," Mom said.
"You might feel sad, mad, or even glad."

Sad

Glad

"It is okay to show
your feelings.
If you are sad,
mad,
or glad,
just show it."

Mad

At school, Cosmos felt sad.
He didn't know what to say to his friends,
because most of them had moms and dads
who were still living together.

"My mom and dad are getting a divorce," he said to Danny.
"Thanks for sharing, Cosmos," Danny replied.
"I feel special that you shared
something so important with me."

Sometimes, Cosmos felt mad.

On the playground, a girl made fun of Cosmos
because his parents were getting a divorce.
Cosmos' mom and dad had talked to him about this
and he knew not to let it bother him.

Cosmos' mom had said, "Sometimes, when people make fun of you, it's because THEY are afraid that THEIR parents might get a divorce."

"It's not because you are weird or bad," his dad told him. "You are still the same person you always were."

Cosmos was surprised to find that lots of the other kids
had moms and dads who were divorced, too.
He was glad he wasn't alone.
"I talked to my Aunt Sue when my parents got divorced,"
Sally told him.

"Who do you have to talk with?" she asked Cosmos.

teacher

friend

relative

Most of his classmates talked to a teacher, a friend, or a relative when their parents divorced. The most important thing, they said, was to talk to someone they could trust to share their true feelings.

"How are you feeling these days, Cosmos?" asked Granny. Cosmos told her he was sad that his mom was moving away. He felt better talking to his grandmother about the divorce.

Cosmos' mom moved to a new apartment when his parents divorced. "Will I get to see you anymore?" Cosmos asked.

Cosmos took some of his toys and clothes to his mom's apartment so he would feel comfortable when he was at her place.

Mom and Dad also helped Cosmos make a calendar that showed the days of the week he would spend at each of their houses.

"Weekdays you're at my house," Dad said. "And weekends you're with me," Mom added.

Cosmos liked Mom's house and Dad's house.

Even though Dad was very busy with work,
he and Cosmos still spent time together every day.

"I'll always have time for you, Cosmos," Dad said.

Mom had things she needed to get done on the weekends.
But she and Cosmos always had fun,
just the two of them.

"I love our special days together," Mom told Cosmos.

Even though they are not married anymore,
Cosmos' parents will always be his parents.

His mom will always be his mom...

...and his dad will always be his dad.

These things never change,
even if his mom and dad do not live together anymore.

But they always told Cosmos one important thing:
"We love you," said Mom.
"Just as much as we always did," said Dad.
"That will never change."

One thing
is for sure!

Your parents
will always be
your parents,

and they
will always
love you,

forever
and ever!

Important Things to Remember if Your Parents Get Divorced

1. It is not your fault that your mom and dad are getting divorced.

2. You cannot do anything to stop your mom and dad from getting divorced, and you cannot make them get back together.

3. Your mom and dad will always be your mom and dad.

4. Make a special time to call the parent you are not staying with to say goodnight.

5. All feelings are okay to have.

6. Talk to someone you trust about your feelings.

7. Ask questions whenever you don't understand something about the divorce.

8. Don't feel embarrassed that your parents are divorced... lots of kids have parents who are divorced.

9. You will always be the same wonderful person, no matter what changes you or your family make.

10. Your mom and dad will always love you!

Draw how you feel today.

MORE THE PLAYDATE KIDS BOOKS
LET'S BE FRIENDS!

Chloe Nova

Chloe gets a new baby brother!

Danny O'Brien

The O'Briens move to a new town.

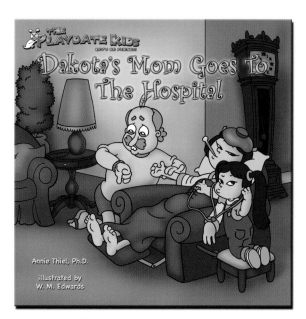

Dakota Greenblatt

Dakota's mom goes to the hospital.

The Playdate Kids

Behavioral themed
coloring and puzzle book
AND animated cartoon DVD set!